RED LINE / BLUE LINE
ICE HOCKEY ADVENTURES

making
the
squad

Library of Congress Catalog Card Number: 73-8188
Standard Book Number: 912022-11-6

Published by AMECUS STREET, 515 North Front Street, Mankato,
Minnesota 56001. An imprint of CREATIVE EDUCATION.

making the squad

by Dennis St. Sauver

AN AMĒCUS STREET BOOK

"Move! Move!", shouted the coach. "Thompson, get the lead out. Halley, pass the puck."

Jeff Kincaid rested against the boards and watched. Last winter he would have been the first guy on the ice and skated on the first line. But moving into a new school district had changed all that. It wasn't that George Hendricks, the coach of the Parkside High Pilots, wasn't fair . . . a coach has to go with the guys he knows can do the job. But Jeff was upset because he knew he could prove he was first line material if given the chance.

Just then Coach Hendricks blew the whistle. "Shake it up guys. Gather 'round here." Jeff hopped over the boards and glided easily to center ice.

"I realize I didn't get you all in today," said the coach, "but you guys who missed out will have your chance

tomorrow when we scrimmage against Riverdale. I'll get a good look at you then. That's all, fellas."

Jeff and Doug Andrews walked slowly home. Doug was a wing on the first line and captain of the Parkside Pilots. He was very popular with his classmates and respected by all of the guys on the team. Jeff liked Doug from the very first day they met at school. Doug introduced himself and invited Jeff to try out for the hockey team.

"You'll get a chance to really show your stuff tomorrow, Jeff," Doug was saying. "And then you won't have any trouble making the team or playing center. Pete Marcus is our first string center. But he gets in trouble at times by playing too rough. He might not be able to hold his position this year and from what I've seen you do with a hockey stick, you may be just the one to fill that spot."

Marcus — called Big Pete by his teammates — was an outstanding hockey player as far as Jeff was concerned. He was a good stick-handler and extremely fast for a big man. But Jeff had noticed that he wasn't too well liked by many of his teammates.

Big Pete was quick to criticize other players and he was also a real hot-head.

Big Pete's size alone made him a terror on the ice. And he caught every chance to show unsuspecting opponents how powerful he was. In today's practice, Big Pete had shaken up two sophomores with illegal checks.

Jeff's side still ached from an elbow Marcus had nailed him with during yesterday's practice.

Jeff had been backchecking on the third line against the first line, which included Big Pete, Doug Andrews, and left winger Bill Hansen. The first line had moved in on a 2 on 1 fast break and Jeff had dropped back to cover up. Big Pete faked a sweep around Jeff but instead very neatly passed the puck over to Bill for what appeared to be a sure goal. Jeff, however, hadn't been fooled by Pete's move and darted in from his wing position to intercept the pass.

The puck cradled on his stick, Jeff had put on a burst of speed and zipped up the ice. He spotted Shorty Sutton, his own center, out of the corner of his eye. He was about to pass the puck across the ice when a sharp pain stabbed his side.

As Jeff recoiled from the blow, he turned to see Big Pete staring at him with a mocking grin. He had caught up with Jeff and had shot his elbow into Jeff's ribs. Jeff had hit the ice from the force of the powerful jab. Gripping his side, he gasped for breath.

In a moment, several players had come over to lend Jeff a hand, apparently not having noticed how it all happened. Then Pete had offered Jeff an outstretched hand while saying: "Need a hand, hot shot?" Jeff leaped up and lunged at him with clenched fists. The other players held him off as Pete turned and skated away.

Just thinking about it now made Jeff burn with anger, but he kept it to himself. It was really just between him and Big Pete.

"Pete's not really a bad guy," continued Doug as they walked along, "but his attitude sure could stand some changing. Don't let him discourage you with all the big talk about how good he is, Jeff. He just wants to let all the newcomers know he's the first line center. He could be a good kid if he'd just quiet down a bit.

"You see, until a few years ago, his father, Stan Mar-

cus, played for the Boston Bears. Pete feels he has a lot to live up to. His dad was the leading scorer in the pro league for two years. Then he was injured in an automobile accident. My dad said he could have been one of the greatest ever to play the game if he hadn't gotten hurt. Most of the guys feel sorry for Pete on account of his dad. That's one reason why nobody says much when he starts mouthing off."

"He was starting to get on my nerves," Jeff admitted. "His remarks about me being a show-off made me mad. He said I should have tried out for another position because center was already taken."

"Well, don't let him get you down," replied Doug. "With your speed and hustle you won't have any trouble making the squad. We have a good team and most of the guys really want to win. We think we have a chance for the city title this year if we can play consistent hockey. Last year we lost in the playoffs to Brady. We were lousy against them. We have almost everybody back this year and we're out to beat Brady and go all the way. With you adding to the team I know we can do it."

They had reached Doug's house and Doug began walking up his driveway.

"I sure appreciate your confidence in me," Jeff told him. "I only hope I can show Coach Hendricks what I can do in that scrimmage tomorrow."

"You will," Doug called back. "See you in the morning."

The following morning, each of Jeff's classes seemed to be lasting for two hours instead of the 50 minutes they actually took up. Jeff's thoughts were mostly on the after-

noon scrimmage. Suddenly, his math teacher's voice interrupted his day-dreaming.

"Jeff Kincaid, will you please come to the board and show the class how to do this equation."

Jeff looked up at Sam Wilson with a startled gaze. He could feel his cheeks warming as the blood surged his face.

"Um, I don't know how to do that one, Mr. Wilson," Jeff said.

"You don't? Well, I assumed since there were no questions regarding the similar one I just finished working that everyone in class understood what to do," said the teacher. "Weren't you paying attention?"

Jeff wondered if it would do any good to try to talk his way out of this one. He decided to take a chance and admit he was daydreaming. This seemed better than appearing to be just plain dumb.

"No, Mr. Wilson," hesitated Jeff. "I was thinking about something else."

"Well," replied his teacher, "maybe you'd better stay after school today and we'll try and concentrate on our algebra at that time."

"But I can't . . . ," blurted Jeff.

"You'll stay, Mr. Kincaid!" And from the expression on Mr. Wilson's face Jeff knew that further discussion was useless.

Jeff slumped miserably at his desk. Of all the things to have happen today! The big scrimmage after school and he was stuck with extra algebra. The bell rang and Mr. Wilson dismissed the class. As Big Pete walked past Jeff, he leaned over and said cheerfully, "Sorry, old buddy.

I'll tell Coach Hendricks you won't be able to make it today. See ya later, smart guy." He walked away, laughing.

The scrimmage got under way and from the very beginning it was obvious that Riverdale was the better hockey team. Their players were bigger and much quicker. By the end of the first period the Pilots were down 5-0 and only the Pilots first and second lines had been skating.

By the time Jeff finished his extra math and got to the practice rink, alongside Parkside's football field, the second period was about to start. He ran up to where the coach was standing. "Coach Hendricks, I'm sorry I'm late, but I had some work to do after school," he said.

"That's okay," replied Coach Hendricks, "at least you have enough determination to show up now. Go get dressed."

When he returned to the rink, Jeff shot a quick glance at Big Pete who was resting on the boards while a third team line was on the ice. Pete's smirk had changed to a look of disgust.

"Kincaid, you'll skate with Andrews and Kapman — get in there on the next face-off," yelled Coach Hendricks. "Let's see some hustle and teamwork out there."

Jeff felt his stomach begin to tighten. Moments later, the referee signaled an offside and skated to the face-off in the Parkside zone. Jeff was watching Riverdale's center, who was several inches taller and weighed much more than he did. Before Jeff realized it, the referee had dropped the puck and Riverdale's right winger was streaking toward the Pilot's net. With a quick move of his head, he deked the Pilots' left defenseman and whirled around him for a shot on goal. Dick Barnett, the Pilot goalie, was

able to get his pad on the shot and he kicked it out in front of the cage.

By this time, Jeff was out front covering up. The puck slid right in front of him. Jeff made a move to cradle the puck and skate up the middle. Before he could act, Riverdale's center swept in, took the puck, and slapped a hard rebound shot into the left corner of the net for a score.

Over the cheers of Riverdale players, Jeff could hear Coach Hendrick's crisp command from rinkside: "Marcus, take over at center."

As Jeff skated over to the bench, Big Pete came by him with a wide, sarcastic grin on his face. "What's the matter, smart guy," Marcus muttered, "is that center position too much for you to handle? Watch and see how it's supposed to be done."

When Jeff reached the boards, Coach Hendricks turned to him. "Kincaid, you can't hesitate like that on a rebound. You have to clear the puck to the side in a hurry. Don't try to be a one-man team. Just pass the darn puck!"

Dejected, Jeff knelt down in the snow behind the boards. His first chance to prove himself and he blew it. He got several other chances before the scrimmage was over but was unable to put anything together. His passes were far off their target and he fanned on two shots out front.

By the time the coaches decided to call the scrimmage, the Pilots were trailing 12-3. Jeff didn't really care about his team's performance. His only concern was how poorly he had played.

He began to worry if he would even make the squad.

There were only two more practices and another scrimmage scheduled before the coach would post the final cut list.

Saturday, the day of the next scrimmage, came very quickly. Jeff had come back with a good practice on Friday. He knew that today was his last opportunity to show Coach Hendricks that he really was good enough to make the team.

Loring Park and Parkside highs were evenly matched, Coach Hendricks pointed out just before the scrimmage was to start. "This will be your last chance to play before I pick the squad for this year," he said. I already have a pretty good idea of who will make it, but a few of you need to show me something yet. Remember, I'm not interested in individual stars. I want team hockey players. Loring is one outfit we can beat if we all work together, so I want to see a real team effort out there today. Okay, let's go."

The coach's remarks recalled for Jeff a chewing out he had received a couple years ago. His coach then had told him to quit trying to be a star and concentrate on team play. His performance had improved when he followed the directive.

He realized that he had again been playing as an individual. He had wanted so much for Coach Hendricks to notice him that he had forgot about teamwork. He was concentrating so hard on "showing off" that his real hockey abilities weren't being demonstrated. Jeff decided to change his approach and he waited anxiously to get onto the ice.

Once again the Pilots started off slow. The defense

was slow covering up and the front line couldn't get the puck across the red line. In the opening minutes Loring had scored two quick goals. Jeff heard Coach Hendricks shout his name and he jumped over the boards so quickly that he almost tripped and fell.

Jeff kept his new aim in mind and on the face-off, he shot the puck quickly to Doug on his right. Then he swiftly advanced toward Loring's goal. His quick action caught the other center off guard and he was able to sweep into the clear for a return pass. Just as Jeff moved to the front of the net, the puck was right in front of him. He wound up and blasted a slap shot right past the open-mouthed Loring goalie.

Jeff's teammates cheered as they lined up for another face-off. Within a couple of minutes the Pilots had

MEADE PARK ELEMENTARY SCHOOL
LEARNING CENTER

scored again to make it 2-2. Jeff's line climbed over the boards as the lines changed and Coach Hendricks patted Jeff on the back and said, "That's the old team-work boys. You really sparked 'em up, Jeff."

Jeff's next opportunity to play came about midway through the final period. Loring had scored again and the Pilots were down 3-2. "Kincaid, Andrews, and Marcus," yelled Coach Hendricks. "Let's see if you three can get this game tied up. Jeff, you'll skate left winger."

Jeff could hardly believe his ears. Skating in the same line with Big Pete! That didn't sound too good.

As Big Pete skated to center Ice, he whispered to Jeff, "Just don't crowd me, hot shot."

Deciding that winning this scrimmage was most important to him right now, Jeff shot back, "Let's just see two goals out there, ace."

Loring controlled the face-off and moved into Park-side's end. The Loring center got free in front of the net and blasted a shot on goal. Dick Barnett kicked the puck to the side, saving another of the many shots the Loring team had gotten off during the scrimmage. Finally, Doug Andrews was able to poke check the puck away from Loring's left winger and began skating up ice.

In a flash, Jeff spotted an opening down the left side of the rink. He darted for it and received a perfect pass from across the ice. When he looked up he saw the Loring defenseman trip and fall.

Now there was nothing between him and Loring's goalie. Jeff streaked toward the center of the net and as he did, he saw Pete also moving in on goal.

With a burst of speed, Jeff cut right in front of Loring's

goalie, drawing him to his left. The goalie covered up the right corner and waited for Jeff's shot. But it was already too late. Jeff had neatly dropped a backhand pass out front, right onto Big Pete's waiting stick. Pete simply flicked the puck into the wide open left corner.

"Great pass, Jeff," yelled Doug as the three skated back to center ice. "That was really smooth."

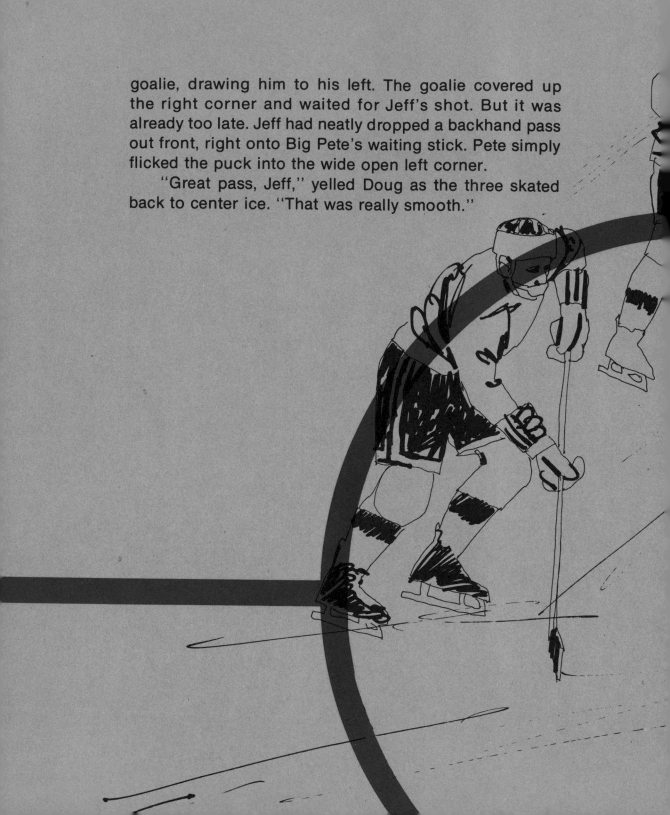

The score was now tied with only two minutes left to play. On the following face-off, Big Pete was able to drop the puck back to a defenseman, who in turn flipped it to Jeff. Jeff rapped the puck off the boards and maneuvered around the opposing winger. The puck bounced back on his stick as he began to move toward the Loring goal.

As he was about to turn, he once again saw Pete skate in front of the goal. Jeff stopped quickly and set himself for a slap shot. Loring's right defenseman moved quickly in front of Jeff in order to block the shot. But instead of shooting, Jeff pushed a pass out in front of Pete, who once again shot it past the Loring goalie. Seconds later, the referee blew the whistle to signal the end of the scrimmage. The Pilot players all dashed out to congratulate Big Pete.

Big Pete turned to Jeff and shot him a grateful smile. Jeff grinned in return and skated over to Doug. The two boys threw their arms around each other and skated off the ice as their teammates patted them on the back.

Jeff crawled over the boards, tired but pleased with his performance. He was pretty sure now that his name would appear on the roster for the Parkside Pilots' hockey team. And he had made at least a temporary truce with Big Pete. They might even get to be friends.

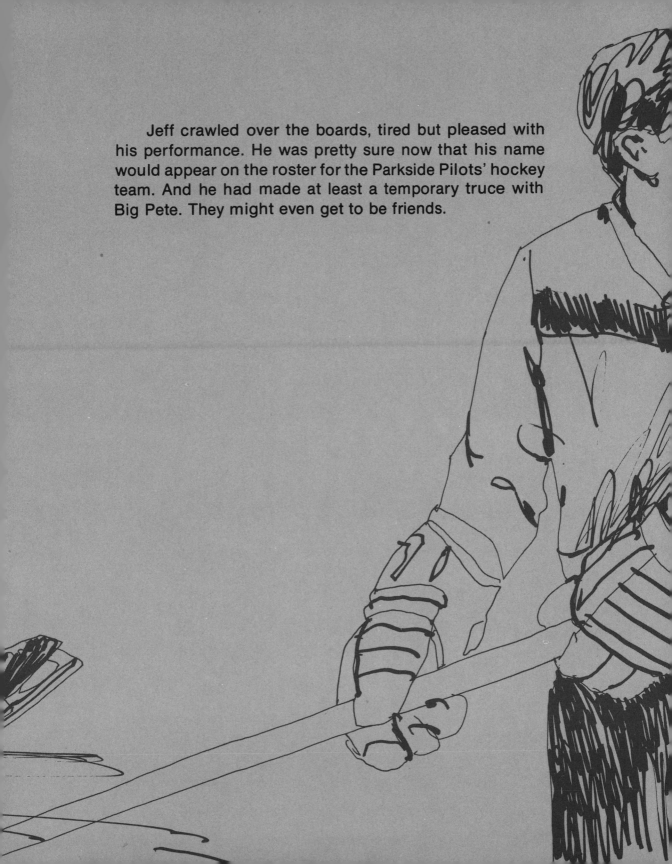

GLOSSARY OF HOCKEY TERMS

Watching a hockey game on TV or reading about games in newspapers or magazines will be more enjoyable if you're familiar with some of the common terms used in the game. Many of these terms are used in this book.

ASSIST: A point awarded to one or more players for taking part in the play leading to the scoring of a goal. The point is for keeping records and is not part of the game score.

BACKHAND: A shot from the "reverse" side of the hockey stick, depending on whether the player ordinarily shoots right or left handed. When a left-hander shoots from his right side, it is a backhand shot.

BLUE LINE: The dividing line between the neutral zone (or "center ice") and the attacking/defensive zone for each team.

BODY CHECK: Hitting an opposing player with your shoulder (shoulder check) or your hip (hip check). The object is to "check" or hinder your opponent's forward progress while in motion.

BREAK: A quick change in direction while skating, most often at high speed.

BREAKAWAY: Used to describe the action of a player carrying the puck when he leads his teammates down the ice or when an attacking player moves in alone on an opposing goal-tender. Also used to describe a quick move with the puck that leaves your opponent behind the play.

CHECK: Another, shorter term for a body check or a poke check. Also can refer to an opposing player a man is assigned to cover.

CLEARING: Used when a player defending his own goal moves the puck out of the area around the goal.

CRISS-CROSS: A common maneuver in offensive play in

which the two attacking wingmen change sides as the play moves down the ice.

DEKE: A fake by the puckcarrier as when close to the opponent's goal, he attempts to bluff the defending goalie into moving first.

FACE-OFF: Hockey play begins when the referee drops the puck between the sticks of two opposing players — as at the start of a game or period. In the face-off the two opponents are positioned face to face, less than a stick length apart.

FAKE SHOT: A trick move in which a player with the puck appears to be getting ready to move, but at the last second continues to carry the puck down the ice.

FIVE ON FOUR: This refers to the situation in which a full team of five players is attacking a team playing one man short. Three on two refers to three forwards attacking two defensemen; two on one describes two offensive players attacking one defensemen. In any of these numerical expressions, the first number tells how many offensive players are involved and the second indicates the number of opposing defensemen (the goaltender is not counted in these instances.) The team with the extra man is said to be on a power play when they control the puck.

FOLLOW-IN: This occurs when a player, after shooting the puck, moves in after his shot to intercept a clearing pass or play a rebound off the boards.

GOAL: The goal is a metal frame, four feet high and six feet wide. It has a cover of netting and is stationary, fixed to the ice.

HAT TRICK: "He scored a hat trick." This means a player scored three goals in one game.

PASSOUT: This refers to a pass by an offensive player from behind the opponent's net or goal to a teammate in front of the net.

PENALTY BOX: A specific seat off the rink and away from players.

POINT: A player receives one point for a goal and one point for an assist.

POKE CHECK: A move to take the puck away from an opposing player or to disrupt his handling of the puck by a one-handed jab or poke at the puck with one's stick.

POWER PLAY: This most commonly refers to an organized attack by a team at full strength against a team playing one or two men short due to penalties.

REBOUND: Shooting the puck against the boards so that it will rebound onto the ice at an angle.

RED LINE: A line across the ice at the exact center of the rink, bisecting the neutral zone between the two blue lines.

SAVE: Any action of the goaltender which keeps a shot on goal out of his net and thus prevents a score by the opposing team.

SCREEN SHOT: Describes a shot made when two or more defending players are between the shooter and the goal.

SHIFT: This refers to a player's or a line's turn on the ice.

SHOOTING ANGLE: Indicates a shooter's position on the ice in relation to the net at the instant he shoots the puck.

SLAP SHOT: A spectacular-looking, though often ineffective, shot in which the shooter draws his stick back — somewhat in the manner of a short back-swing in golf — and brings it down into the puck and on through. A shooter seldom scores with a slap shot, since the motion doesn't allow for much accuracy or control of direction in which the puck will travel.

SMOTHERING: This refers to when a player, usually a goalie, falls on the puck.

STICK LIFT: A defensive move in which a defensive player, skating close to the attacking puck-carrier, lifts his opponent's stick from the ice by hooking it at the heel with his own stick.